Weirdo

BEN SPIES

Weirdo

ILLUSTRATED BY ROBERT SPIES

Spies Publishing

First self-published in paperback in New Zealand 2015

This edition published in New Zealand in 2018
Paraparaumu Beach, Kapiti Coast 5032

Ben Spies' website address is
www.benspies.weebly.com

Written © by Ben Spies 2015, 2016, 2017
Illustrated © by Robert Spies 2015, 2016, 2017
Published by Spies Publishing Limited
All rights reserved.

Ben Spies and Robert Spies assert the moral right to be
identified as the author and illustrator of this work respectively.

ISBN 978-0-473-42495-4

Typesetting by Vida and Luke Kelly.

To Mum and Dad,
I love you.

WEIRDO

Once there was a boy called Ugine, and he was going to experience a big change in his life . . . But first, you need to know a little bit about him.

He was a nice chap but, well, he was . . . a weirdo!

Yep, you heard me. A right, proper weirdo. But with great weirdness comes great responsibility, curiosity and, of course, lots and lots of fun.

RING! RING!
RING!

School had started and Ugine was not looking forward to it. Everyone made fun of him because he was weird. No one likes being treated like that and he hated it.

First up was algebra class. He ended up getting an F minus. Then he had spelling class. This time he got an F plus. A little bit better but then he got an F minus in his reading class. He left feeling ashamed, like he was no good at anything.

As he walked out of the classroom he bumped into a girl and spilled all her drink.

'Oh! Sorry!' Ugine said.

'ARGHHH!' the girl screamed. 'I've got weirdo germs! **ARGHHH!'**

Everyone watching started to scream or shout and run away.

Ugine just sat down and started crying.

Now, you may be thinking—Why is Ugine weird? Well, let's go back a few weeks . . .

'As you know, the square root of 38,987 is . . . Yes, Ugine?' asked the algebra teacher.

'A pork chop,' Ugine answered.
'What? No. It's not a pork chop.'

'What about a pie?'
'No.'
'A clock?'
'No. Ugine!'
'A stapler?'
'What did I say the first time? NO!' the teacher replied, losing her patience. That was the last straw. **'OOOOOOOOOOOOOOO UUUUUUUT!'** she shouted.

'Oh, okay.' Ugine sighed and left the room.

Now this isn't really weird, but that's just for starters . . .

'Goop, come here boy,' called Ugine one morning.

Ugine was outside his house, standing on the front porch wearing his old, worn-out pyjamas. His dog had somehow escaped.

'Come here, Goop!' (that was his dog's name).

'Come on!' Ugine sighed.

But Goop was a little deaf so he thought 'Goop' was 'poop' and pooped on the spot.

'Oh! Goop!'

Ugine couldn't leave the house or he would be seen in his PJs.

Then, Goop made a run for it.

'What? **NO! GOOOOOOOOOOP!**' Ugine shouted.

Now Ugine didn't have a choice. He had to catch Goop. As Goop ran through the neighborhood he barked like mad. Everyone was going to wake up and see Ugine!

'WOOF! WOOF!'

'Goop! Stop!' Ugine shouted, just before skidding on Goop's poo. *'Whoaaaaaahhhh!'* he cried, falling backward. 'Uhhhhh!'

Then he realised there was a crowd of people surrounding him in disgust. Even worse, they were all from his school.

'Oops, I had a wee little a–a–a–accident,' he chuckled nervously.

'Aaaaaaaaaaaaaaaaa aaaaaaaaaaaaaaaaaaaa aaaaaaaaaaaaaaaaaaaa aaaaaaaaaaaaaaaa aaaaaaaaaaaaaaaaa aaaaaaaaaaaaaaaaaaa aargh!' everyone screamed.

They quickly scattered, leaving him on the street with a dog which smelled like a poo.

Well, it was actually Ugine who was the smelly one!

Now, you may be wondering about Ugine's family. Well, he didn't have one. His mum died when he was born and then it was only him and his dad. But then, one night, someone broke in and stole all their money and credit cards. They soon became poor and his dad got very ill and sadly passed away. Ugine now owned the house but no one knew. He had to keep it a secret. It was his only chance of survival. He had to learn to live by himself, so he scavenged the streets for money. That's when Ugine found Goop and took him in. As well as being poor he didn't have any friends. Well, except for one. Now that you know everything about him we can get back to the story.

Ugine isn't very intelligent but only because he goes to a bad school. So he doesn't know many things. Here's an example—it's fruit-break time and he has a banana. He notices that Billy has one, too. He pretends he is phoning Billy with a banana which is awkward, right? Yep, it is!

So, on with the story . . . where was I? Ah yes . . .

'Doo, doo, da, da, do, da, da, doooo . . .' a boy in the street sang one of The Maxwell Brothers' tunes.

Ugine was outside the shop of the one and only person who cared about him—Kal. He was a newsagent who owned a rather scruffy shop. Just around the corner was a little boy who sang really well. He was around Ugine's age, ten. The boy only had five bucks in his busking hat. Luckily, he wasn't from Ugine's school. Ugine only had three dollars but he felt sorry for the kid, so he put one dollar in the boy's hat. The kid looked at him and smiled. Ugine smiled back.

WEIRDO

Kal's shop smelled like a dump and it looked like a bomb had exploded inside.

Ugine went up to the counter. 'Hi Kal,' he said.

'Oh! Hi Ugine. What have you been up to today?' Kal asked.

'Oh, you know. Not much, as usual.'

'Righto. So, what would you like today?'

'Uh . . . have you got anything for two bucks?' Ugine asked, looking at the last of his money.

'Yes, we do. Well, me, not we,' Kal chuckled. 'Right this way.'

'So?' Ugine said.

'So what?' Kal asked.

'. . . We're outside the shop.'

'Oh! Back inside then.'

'Um . . . why are we in the freezer now?' Ugine asked.

'Freezer? What freezer?'

'This freezer!' Ugine shouted, getting annoyed.

'Oh yeah! My bad.'

Then Ugine remembered that Kal was a little blind.

Oops, thought Ugine, feeling sorry for his friend as they left the freezer.

'Here you go,' Kal passed him a bag of bread free-of-charge.

'Whoa? Are you sure?' Ugine said.

Kal smiled. 'I'm sure.'

Okay, so you get the idea that Ugine is a little weird but very kind hearted? Pardon? Yes? Oh, good.

The main reason everyone thinks he's weird is because of the last school assembly. It didn't go that well for Ugine and here's why . . .

~~~~~~

Blah Blah Blah Blah Blah Blah Blah...

Mr. Morrison took forever to finish talking about sports. He went on and on.

You would think that a PE teacher would be fit but actually he was fat. Really fat. Once he got stuck in a doorway. His voice was muffled, too. So when he screamed for help, no one understood and he was stuck there overnight. Even now when he talks about sports nobody understands. So now basically no one plays sports.

Finally, he was finished.

The principal stepped onto the stage.

'And now it's time to announce the winner of this year's Science Fair . . .' he said.

Ugine's eyes lit up. This is it, he thought, hoping his name would be called out.

The principal brought out the note which would reveal the winner.

'And the winner is . . . Steven!'

'YES!' Steven shouted. 'YES!'

Ugine clapped disappointedly. 'Good job, Steven,' he still managed to say.

Steven looked at him. 'And what have you ever won?' he said meanly.

'Um . . .' Ugine tried to think.

'My fist!' Steven shouted and punched Ugine in the stomach.

'Ouch! That hurt,' Ugine cried.

Upset, he quickly tried to leave assembly, but accidentally tripped Steven up.

'Arghhh!' Steven shouted as he fell to the floor. He chipped his tooth. Everyone stared at Ugine.

'YOU PEA-BRAINED WEIRDO!' shouted a mean kid.

'YEAH! WEIRDO!' shouted another.

'WEIRDO, WEIRDO, WEIRDO!'

shouted another and another and another.

Now, do you get why they think he's a weirdo? Well, that's why. So let's get back to the "story story" at school.

~~~~~~

(Sniff) 'It's not fair, all I said was good job and now everyone hates me,' cried Ugine.

RING! RING! RING!

Lunch break was over.

'I'm going home,' Ugine said and off he went.

Everyone was scurrying to get back to class, but Ugine wasn't. He was going home. He bumped into Steven and his friends on the way.

'Hey, it's you!' Steven said.

'Oh no . . .' Ugine backed away.

'So we meet again. It will cost about 100 bucks to pay for my tooth filling,' Steven said.

'How would you feel if your parents had to pay that?'

Ugine thought for a moment . . . he didn't have any parents. 'Um . . .'

'It's a rhetorical question, dumbo,' Steven said.

'HEY! Break it up kids!' shouted a teacher.

'Catch you later,' shouted Steven. 'And I mean catch.'

They all ran away.

'Humph,' the teacher said and left.

That went well, Ugine thought to himself and walked off.

zzzzzzzzzz

~~~

That night Ugine gazed up at the stars. Well, he wanted to. Instead he looked up and saw the ceiling. He turned and sighed. Then he fell asleep . . .

zzzzzzzzzzzzzzzzzzZZZZZZZ

WEIRDO

ZZZZZZZZZZZZZ...

'WOOF! WOOF! WOOF!'

Goop barked.

'What now?' Ugine called.

It was the middle of the night and Ugine could smell smoke. **'GOOP? GOOP? WHERE ARE YOU?'**

Ugine shouted, spotting an orange glow.

'Oh no!' he said. 'It can't be!' He ran down the stairs and he had guessed right, it was a fire. **'Noooooo!'** Ugine shouted. Then he remembered that Goop's cage was in the laundry. Ugine rushed down the stairs like mad.

What started the blaze? he wondered.

The flames grew higher and higher. He couldn't get to the laundry. He feared Goop would die. Then the stairs started to catch fire. The way up was blocked by flames and

the way down was in flames. He was trapped.
The staircase was ablaze, it was going to fall!
He heard a cracking noise and the stairs gave
way. Ugine fell to his doom, this was the end
for him.

'AAAAARGHHHHHH!'

he shouted.

He closed his eyes and . . .

Kal smashed through the wall wearing a tuxedo, holding onto a rope and grabbed Ugine. He was about a second away from his death but Ugine was saved just in time.

'KAL! What are you doing?'

'Saving you, duh.'

Ugine smiled. Kal smiled back.

They escaped the building quickly. Then Ugine remembered Goop!

'What about Goop?' he screamed.

'Oh God!' Kal said, jumping onto the rope. 'I'll be back . . . hopefully.' And with that he swung into the blazing house.

All of a sudden Ugine heard a **WOOF!**

'GOOP!' he cheered merrily. 'You're alive!'

Kal came swinging back.

'And I am, too!' Kal said.

They sat down on the roof of the house next door and watched Ugine's house burn down.

'Where will I live now?' Ugine asked.

'With me,' Kal answered, smiling happily.

'Really?' said Ugine excitedly.

'Of course.'

'By the way, why are you wearing a tuxedo?' Ugine asked.

'Oh, I thought this was my everyday clothing,' Kal said.

'Since when did you own a tuxedo?'

'Um, about eight years ago.'

'WHAT?' Ugine said.

'It's a long story. I'll tell you one day . . .'

'It's on the news,' Kal shouted.

'I know,' Ugine replied. 'And now the authorities know that I lived there. What if they fine me for lying? I can't pay that sort of money. It's too much!'

'Don't worry, I'll pay it,' Kal said. 'I look after you now, remember?'

'Gee thanks, Kal,' Ugine said, giving him a bear-hug.

ONE YEAR LATER . . .

Life was good for Ugine. He had been adopted by Kal and was now going to a good school, which meant he was much cleverer. He had a ton of friends, plenty of food, clean water and awesome toys. He was like an ordinary boy.

Ugine also helped Kal out in the shop and had saved enough money to help Kal fix his eyes; now he can see properly.

If you are a weirdo and think that's bad, don't worry, it just means you're going to have one heck of an adventure.

The End

For Daniel,

The most annoying
brother ever.

Weirdo

(2)

The Brazilian
Adventure

Yes, that's right, I'm back. My name is Ugine. I've had many adventures and this is going to be the best one yet! And the deadliest! Stay tuned to hear about crocodile attacks, deadly poachers, giant water rapids and more!

'So,' the teacher said. 'Now that you all know about Brazil we can go on our field trip tomorrow.'

Everyone in Ugine's class cheered. They'd all just been told about the place they were going to.

'YAY!'

Oops, sorry, I haven't told you about Ugine. Well, he's had a hard life, but now he is really happy with his adoptive father—Kal.

Ugine had started at a new school and was going on a field trip to south Brazil. They were going to Iguacu Falls—a collection of about 275 waterfalls!

Ugine thought about Kal as he walked home. Kal was going to be lonely. Ugine and his class were leaving on the 23rd July, two days before Kal's birthday. He had already agreed that Ugine could go.

Ugine arrived at Kal's shop. He was greeted by a semi-warm smile.

'Hi Kal,' Ugine said.

'Hi,' replied Kal in a gloomy tone.

Ugine knew there was something wrong. 'What's happened?' Ugine asked.

'Well, you know . . . You're not going to be here for my birthday.'

'Don't worry. I'll only be away for three days.'

Kal seemed to smile but it quickly faded away.

Now all I have to do is wait until tomorrow, Ugine thought to himself as he climbed up the stairs to his bedroom. He slumped down onto his bed and fell fast asleep . . .

'WOOF! WOOF! WOOF!'

'What . . . ?' Ugine had slept for twelve hours! His dog Goop was barking at the end of his bed.

'Hello Goop,' Ugine said. 'What are you doing?'

Goop pointed his head at the alarm clock. Ugine looked at it. He felt like he was going to scream! It was ten past ten! The plane to Brazil was due to leave at eleven o'clock!

Ugine rushed out of his bedroom and sped down the stairs into the shop.

'KAL!' Ugine shouted.

Startled, Kal dropped a drink he was serving to a customer. The drink hit the floor, splashing all over the customer.

'AHEM, this is unacceptable!' the customer yelled, storming out of the shop.

'Kal, I want to say good-bye,' Ugine said.

Kal immediately remembered that Ugine had to go. He ran over to Ugine and gave him the biggest bear-hug ever.

'I love you,' he said.

'I love you, too,' Ugine replied.

'I'll be thinking of you. Be safe.' Kal reached for Ugine's hand.

'Don't worry,' Ugine said. 'I'll be totally safe.'

But Ugine was wrong. He was nowhere close to being safe . . .

The plane was starting up. This was it. Ugine was going to travel to another country for the first time! He sat next to the person he trusted the most—the teacher. Her name was Boosger, make that, Mrs. Boosger. He was in the middle of two people, his teacher and a complete stranger. The stranger looked like a punk. He was listening to a song with his headphones on.

'La la la la la la la la la, ooh ooh hahoo, oh yeah,' the punk dude sang.

He noticed Ugine looking at him.

'Hey, mind your own business, man!'

One: Ugine was not a man.

And two: he was minding his own business!

It was a long trip but eventually they arrived at their destination. They got off the plane. Mrs. Boosger made sure everyone was there. They formed a line and walked to the cabs. It must have been stressful for Mrs. Boosger to look after all the children. They got into their cabs and sped off to Iguacu Falls!

Ugine wasn't with any adults in the cab except the driver. In the cab with him was: Max, a sort of bully-like person; Simon, a complete nerd; Goof, a crazy weird guy (you can tell by his name); and finally, Claire. She is a girl. Everyone in the car was excited about the falls, especially at the fact that they were higher than Niagara Falls!

By now they could see the dense deep-green jungle and their hotel. All the other cabs were already there in the hotel car park. Goof was annoyed that they were last so he screamed into the driver's ear.

'HURRY UP!'

The driver got a fright.

'AAAAARRGHHHH!' he screamed.

He swerved the car to the side, smashing through the fence near the edge of the road. They drove off the road, and the cab plunged down the mountainside.

BEN SPIES

The driver started cursing. Ugine felt like crying. He was way too young to die! He thought about Kal, about his dog Goop, about his life. Then everything went black . . .

~~~

First came light. Then the sound of water. Ugine stood up. He'd survived. It was a miracle! The car had landed on the river bank. Ugine looked up. It was a long way to the top. He looked around him. Max was nowhere to be seen, nor was Goof. Suddenly, Max jumped out at Ugine from behind. Ugine jumped a foot into the air.

'Hah,' Max chuckled.

Goof was with him.

'You guys are alive!' Ugine said.

'Yeah, of course we are,' Goof replied.

Ugine looked over at Claire and Simon.

'Are they alive?'

'Yes,' replied Max. 'But they're not awake yet.'

'What about the driver?' Ugine asked.

'We're not sure,' answered Goof, 'we can't find him.'

~~~~~~~~

'This thing is so heavy,' Ugine complained, trying to move the car closer to the water.

'Well, just lift it!' Max said.

'Simon woke up! Simon woke up!' Goof screamed at the top of his voice.

Everyone hurried over to Goof. Simon was awake. Then Claire started twitching, she was waking up, too.

'We're all alive! It's a miracle!' shouted Simon.

Suddenly, they heard a grunting noise behind them.

'Not for long though!' said Simon.

'RUN LIKE THE WIND!'

Claire screamed.

The others turned around.

CROCODILE!

The croc launched itself at them.

'We're all gonna be crocodile food if we don't scram!'

At those words, they all scrammed, only to face the mountainside! They had reached a dead end. The crocodile came closer and closer. Its humongous tail hit the car pushing it exactly to where Ugine wanted. Now they could move it into the water and float away from the deadly crocodile. Ugine quickly told his plan to the others and they ran over to the car. The crocodile did not like that and started chasing them.

Ugine and the others pushed the car into the water and hopped on top of it. They were balancing on a floating car in the middle of the river! The crocodile slid into the water. It was swimming closer.

'Go faster!' Goof screamed.

Then they hit the rapids.

The car bashed into the rocks. The five of them held on for dear life. The water was getting faster and whiter.

'Yay. We're white water rafting!' Claire shouted over the noise.

All of a sudden, their enemy jumped up onto the back of the car.

'ARGHHHH! HE'S BACK!'

cried Ugine.

The crocodile must have been a girl, because it definitely didn't like the word "he".

Max looked around. 'And this time she's brought friends,' he said.

The others looked around too. He was right, she had brought friends! They heard something they would never want to hear again . . . the noise of a waterfall.

'We're heading straight for the Iguacu Falls!' Simon shouted.

The water got shallower and the car stopped, stuck between the rocks! The children had nowhere to go and the crocodiles were going crazy trying to catch them. They would have to jump.

'What do we do now?' Ugine asked.

With no hesitation, Claire jumped down the waterfall. Deliberately. The others looked down. She was hanging on a branch sticking out from the cliff side.

The rest all jumped just before the crocodiles could take a bite out of them. They all clung to the branch.

'If only I could swing over there,' Claire said.

The others looked to the tree she was pointing at. Suddenly, they heard a dreadful cracking noise. The branch was snapping!

'Quick! Swing!' everyone shouted to Claire.

She swung over to the tree, followed by Goof and Max.

Before Ugine and Simon could swing over, the branch broke and they fell onto a pile of leaves just below the tree. It was soft but it still hurt a lot. They looked over at how close they were to the waterfall edge. Then they saw the car falling, smashing into the rocks down below.

The car exploded. Pieces of metal flew everywhere.

'Take cover!' Ugine screamed to Simon.

The others in the tree watched as the action unfolded below. 'Nice fireworks display,' Max said.

WEIRDO 2

Right at that moment, they heard a gunshot. Ugine hid behind a log and Simon ducked behind a tree. A jaguar burst out into the open. Ugine could see its fascinating teeth and golden fur. Then a horrible thing happened. A poacher came out of nowhere and shot the poor creature. The jaguar fell and slowly died. Simon started trembling making some leaves fall from the tree above.

The poacher spotted Simon hiding and picked him up. 'You're coming with me.'

Simon started to squeal like a pig.

'Help me, Ugine!' he shouted.

The poacher dropped Simon and found Ugine.

'I knew there were two of you,' he said.

The other three saw the whole thing from up high.

'Quickly, we've got to save them!' whispered Claire, climbing down the tree.

They raced through the jungle trying to save the others.

'Get in there, you dirty little kids.'

The poacher threw the kids into a jail made of bamboo.

'That's what you get for spying on me,' he said and left the room.

'Ugine, I'm scared,' Simon said.

'There's nothing to be worried about,' Ugine said. 'I'll just bust us out.'

But as hard as he tried he would never be able to bust anybody out.

Back in the forest Max, Goof and Claire tried to survive in the tropical heat.

'HELP ME! I'M MELTING, I'M MELTING!' Goof moaned.

Right then, Max tripped over a rock and came face-to-face with a snake. A coral snake to be exact! Its bright colors shone in Max's eyes. Red, yellow, black... then a voice started up like an engine.

'MAX! RUUUUUUUUUN!'

Max woke up from his daze and got up.

The snake striked at him and Max dove into the leaves. He could see his friends in the distance. He sprinted like hell but the coral snake was not far away. Its long body slithered toward him. Max ran into a spider web. It stuck all over his face.

'HELP MEEEE!!!!'

he screamed.

Claire picked up a stick with a sharp pointy end. Max was on the floor, screaming for help. The coral snake slithered onto his body. Did I mention they are highly poisonous? Claire threw the stick right at the snake. The sharp bit stabbed the snake's skin—I don't know what bits of the body the snake has, it's all just skin to me—and the snake fell off Max. But now they had bigger problems.

~~~~~~

'Somebody let us out of here!' Ugine shouted.

'I need water,' Simon groaned.

'How about we cheer ourselves up by telling some jokes?' Ugine suggested.

'Okay,' Simon replied. 'You go first.'

'What do you call a cow that lives underground?'

'Don't know,' Simon said.

'Ground beef!'

Simon just stood there. Not a smile to be seen.

'Okay, what about this one,' suggested Ugine, 'why did the picture go to jail?'

'Don't know,' Simon said again.

'Cause it got framed!'

Instead of laughing, Simon burst out crying.

'What's the matter?' Ugine asked.

'You told a joke about jail and we **ARE** in jail! *Waaaa waaaa! Wah wah wahhhhh!*'

'Here we go again,' Ugine said.

MEANWHILE, IN THE FOREST . . .

'Guys! It's creeping up my leg!'

Max was really freaking out. Can you guess why? Well, because there was a Brazilian wandering spider crawling up his leg. One tiny little bite could kill him instantly.

'I don't think it's happy that I broke its web,' Max said.

Claire grabbed another stick. 'Max, stay still. I'm gonna whack it.'

'What is it with you and sticks?' Goof said.

'Uh, nothing,' she said in the most girlish voice ever.

By now the spider was edging its way toward Max's belly button.

WEIRDO 2

Claire slowly raised the stick and then brought it down very fast, but she wasn't fast enough. The spider saw what was happening and jumped out of the way. So, instead of hitting the spider, Claire hit Max where it really hurts for a boy.

'OOOOOOOHHH, YOUCH!'

Max was about to faint. The spider crawled away.

Hopefully, never to return . . .

'Will anything break these bars?' grunted Simon. 'Anything? I mean, like, they are only bamboo, right?'

'Simon, we've got to get out of here and call the police. Those poachers are killing jaguars only for their fur!' Ugine said.

'But how are we gonna get out?' Simon replied.

'Well, we'll just have to rely on the others, won't we?'

~~~~~

'I'm thinking that's where the poachers are,' Goof said, pointing to the camp.

They walked toward the building. It was a mess everywhere!

'Their home is a total dump!' Claire said. 'There are hardly any plants here.'

Right at that moment, Claire fell over face-first to the ground. Goof chuckled.

'Well, there's a face-plant!' He burst out laughing. Max did, too.

'Ha ha ha, so funny!' Claire said. 'Not! How are we going to get past the guards?'

Just as she asked, they saw a little monkey coming down from a tree.

'Hmm . . . I think I know,' Max said.

'Ooh ooh, aah aah!' the little monkey chattered.

'Aww, it's so cute,' said one of the guards.

While the guards were distracted, the kids slipped into the dirty old building. They came to a door which said . . .

KEEP OUT!
GO AWAY!

'Maybe we should go away . . .' Goof suggested.

'Maybe we should go in!' Claire said, opening the door.

They snuck in. There were jaguar skins and other stuffed animals hanging on the walls.

'These people are going to pay for what they did to those poor animals!' Claire said.

They quickly sneaked out of the room and walked down a corridor. If one of the poachers caught them, they would be poached—get it? Poached.

They came to another door which said . . .

PRISON

'They should be in here,' Max said.

They opened the door. Inside there were lots of innocent people and other poachers who had been captured for betrayal.

'Come on, let's find Simon and Ugine quickly,' Claire said.

They looked everywhere. There were old men on the floor, clawing at the bars, hoping to be saved too. Eventually, they found their friends.

Ugine was so relieved. 'You saved us! Let's go before the guards come back!' he said.

They ran out of the prison, down the corridor and out into the jungle again. Two angry guards stood outside. Make that three. No, four! Four angry guards!

'Get them!' screamed one of the guards.

'Run!' Ugine shouted.

The guards spread out. Max ran into a swampy area.

'Oh no . . .' he whispered under his breath.

A crocodile started swimming toward the poacher.

'ARGHHH!' the poacher shouted.

The crocodile attacked him, knocking him down into the water. Max got to the other side of the swamp safely. Claire climbed into a tree. The other poacher reached the bottom of the tree.

'Where is that little brat?' he said.

Claire got angry and snapped a big branch off the tree.

The poacher looked up. It bonked him right on the head. Goof ran back to the poachers' camp hoping they wouldn't expect him to return but a poacher found him. Goof backed away. Then he had an idea.

'Look!' he shouted. 'A unicorn!'

It was pretty unbelievable that the poacher actually looked. Goof took the advantage and ran toward the poacher. He performed some deadly moves he had learned in his karate lessons. The poacher fell down in pain.

'Oh yeah!' Goof said.

Ugine jumped over a log. Simon followed behind but so did the last poacher. Ugine grabbed a vine.

'Simon, grab it!' Ugine threw the vine to Simon.

Simon grabbed one side of the vine and hid in the bushes. The poacher came closer and tripped over the vine.

'WHHHAAAA!' he screamed. The poacher got up. 'Where are you little rascals?' he said.

Then Simon sneezed.

'A-A-ACHOO!'

The poacher looked Ugine's way, his mouth wide open. All of Simon's snot was in the poacher's mouth!

'UGHHHHH!'

In disgust, the poacher stumbled into the swamp. His head didn't bob up. Not once.

All the children got back together.

'We've got to get back to the hotel!' Ugine said.

'But how? We're in a valley!' Goof asked.

'Well, we've got to climb out of it!' Max suggested.

Claire didn't say a word. It seemed like she was thinking. Then her eyes sparkled.

'Back at the poachers' place there was a helicopter,' she said, 'maybe if we sneak in again we'll be able to start it up!'

'Good idea, let's get moving,' Ugine said.

Back at the camp, the children sneaked up onto the roof of the building. There it was! The helicopter stood in all its glory but, even better, there were no guards. They climbed into the helicopter.

'Hold on, does anyone know how to fly this thing?' asked Simon.

'My dad does!' Goof shouted. 'And he

taught me how!'

Everyone looked at Goof. Nobody wanted him to fly . . . (because he's goofy!!). Then they heard a gunshot. The bullet bounced off the side of the helicopter.

'GO GO GO GO!' everyone screamed.

Goof started the engine up and the helicopter rose from the roof. Ugine looked down at the poachers. He realised something was different. One of them was wearing a different uniform and he had a pin that said **BOSS**.

B as in best

O as in owesome (obviously this guy didn't know how to spell awesome)

S as in super, and

S as in skilled.

This guy was the boss of the poachers!

He jumped up and hung onto the landing gear while still holding his gun. Gunshots came from the jungle. The poachers were shooting at them! The boss clung on to the helicopter for dear life.

'Try to shake him off!' Claire said.

A little tune started in Simon's head. He began to sing and I can tell you it was horrible but it seemed like the boss hated it even more!

'. . . Shake, shake, shake, shaky, shaky, shaky, shake shake, shaky, shakyyyyyyyy . . .'

So on and so on. It was torture! But eventually the boss had enough. He let go.

'CURSES!' he shouted.

And that was the last they ever saw of him.

Soon after, they landed safely outside the hotel. Their whole class was waiting for them. Everyone ran over to them to hear about what had happened. Ugine looked at them and then collapsed in exhaustion.

———

He woke up at the airport back home. The first thing he saw was Kal.

'Kal!'

'Ugine! Are you alright?'

They hugged each other tightly.

'I was so worried about you!' Kal said.

'Me too!'

'I'm never letting you go on another field trip again!'

Ugine smiled. *For my own safety* . . . he thought.

Then Ugine remembered something.

'Happy Birthday!' he said to Kal.

Kal was so happy. 'Thank you, Ugine.'

'I was only away for two days in the end ...'

When Ugine arrived home, Goop ran up to him.

'Hello Goop!' Ugine said.

'GOOP!' barked Goop.

'Goop talked! He said his name!' said Ugine excitedly.

Well, it seemed like it was going to be Ugine's happy day after all ...

That, my friend, was the biggest event in Ugine's life. He had a humongous adventure. And I think he's growing out of being a weirdo.

Maybe ...

The End

Take a tour at Ben's official website and
find out more about his upcoming books!

www.benspies.weebly.com

Also by Ben Spies:
The Magic Pencil

Discover:
www.spiespublishing.co.nz

Made in the USA
Columbia, SC
21 July 2022